L Bennett

AuthorHouse™
1663 Liberty Drive
Bloomington, IN 47403
www.authorhouse.com
Phone: 1 (800) 839-8640

Published by AuthorHouse

ISBN: 978-1-5462-0463-3 (sc)
ISBN: 978-1-5462-0462-6 (e)

Library of Congress Control Number: 2017912619

Print information available on the last page.

Any people depicted in stock imagery provided by Thinkstock are models,
and such images are being used for illustrative purposes only.
Certain stock imagery © *Thinkstock.*

This book is printed on acid-free paper.

Because of the dynamic nature of the Internet, any web addresses or links contained in this book may have changed
since publication and may no longer be valid. The views expressed in this work are solely those of the author and do not
necessarily reflect the views of the publisher, and the publisher hereby disclaims any responsibility for them.

authorHOUSE

Author Biography

Amanda Bennett is a born and raised country girl who calls Calgary, Alberta her home. She is an entrepreneaur driven career woman with a passion for writing and a true sense of fulfillment when spending time with her loved ones.

Dedication

I dedicate this bedtime story to my one and only son, Sterling, who inspired me to begin writing this 20 years ago and to his precious daughter, Tessa, who inspired the completion so that he can read it to her when he tucks her in and kisses her goodnight.

Hush little one for night time is near

Where the stars twinkle bright
Glittering gems in the atmosphere

Lay as still as you can and
let your eyelids fall down
Sink into pillowy softness; as if
floating high above the ground

While I gently glide my finger
from your forehead to your nose
You fall slowly into
unconsciousness where every
little piece of you grows

For about to begin is a
most wonderful ride
A perfect adventure where
all your dreams come alive

Now it's time to let your
imagination take flight
As I place you down gently and
tuck you in nice and tight

With a tender kiss goodnight
and a final glance from above
I make a wish for you my child
and seal it with my love

Sweet dreams little one,
for the day is now done
I will await your beautiful
smile, when we can begin
another day of fun

CPSIA information can be obtained
at www.ICGtesting.com
Printed in the USA
LVOW06s1210070917
547657LV00010BA/25/P

9 781546 204633